CHAPTER ONE

INTRODUCTION

Life is like a smoke in the fire for him. When it goes no one knows as he was also going out like a smoke. Though want to live life to the fullest but destiny has not given so much time for that. But it was a dream to be in top and he is fulfilling that and would fulfill that, as it is said "the biggest adventure you can take is to live the life of your dreams". Though he had no regret out of life but sometime he thinks if it was not be like that then his life would have been different. He would definitely have been in some industry even without higher education and if that would have happened, he would have got his love too. But then the life would have been without any adventure. It is just an imagination, everyone imagines the life to be different than the way it is. I am not the philosopher, not a story writer even but a technical person authoring the life of a person and imagining it to be different than what it is. The purpose of this story is to express the agonies faced by him in love and the way he wants to live life but destiny has not allowed him to do so. This strange but true love story is written by heart, but at the end of the story he is satisfied that at least he experienced the most beautiful thing in the world, that is the love. Absence makes the heart grow fonder. He still loves his beloved and is in tears on remembering the time spent with her, he still waits for her and when is in a sad mood remembers her and even sends her message whether she reads it or not. It is believed that as we grow in strength in our spiritual life, we give up the habit of worrying. It serves no purpose other than to make us feel tense and miserable. If I stop fretting about things that are beyond my control and rather focus on generating optimistic and kind thoughts, my life can begin to flow in more positive directions. Such a light and easy approach to life enables me to take everything in my stride. But this approach is hypothetical rather than realistic for him. The story starts at this stage which is truly heartening and I as an author of the story would not be able to present the whole picture of the story if I do not imagine myself to be in his place.

CHAPTER TWO

THE SADDEST TIME OF MY LIFE

The saddest time of my love "Falling in love is awfully simple, but falling out of love is simply awful" It was the 3rd April 2009 at 8:34 PM, I received a message from my school time friend Sonam "I am going to United States today, I will talk to you once I reach there, take care". I was in deep thought as what she wants to tell me, as she never sends me message like that. It seems something very urgent and may be it is concerned with my life. She was my school time friend and married to a software engineer. She was working in a software company in Delhi. As her husband had been transferred to US and she was going to join him there. It seems that the message had been sent from airport only. Next day was a usual day for me. I simply forgot about her message too. At around 8:30 PM she gave me a call and said "Hi Sameer, how are you? I was in hurry that day so I simply sent you a message, because I was boarding flight to US. I want to tell you something which seems to be very important in your life". I was excited "What? Please tell me, I am dying to hear what you want to say." She replies "I had been in Jammu for few days. I met Sonia"s sister. She is going to marry in the mid April and she was busy in preparations for the same. Please forget about her as she is going to be someone else"s wife now". I became mute for a moment. It seemed as if someone has taken heart away from my body, as if I was a body without soul, a warrior defeated in the battle of life. I was in tears, my heartbeat increased and it seemed as if my heart will come out of my body. She asked me, "Are you there Sameer? What has happened to you? Are you alright?" "Yeah, I am alright. When is she going to be married and what her fiancé do?" I asked in great despair. "Well I don"t know more details about that, but Sonia works in a Delhi and her fiancé is also in Delhi and also he is from southern part of India" She replied. It reminded me of her reluctance to talk to her family on the basis of caste as in her view her family had orthodox views in matters related to caste. But, what about her marriage to a person, who was not only of different caste but belonged to a very different 3 culture also. Why her orthodox family did not object to her marriage with that boy. I have many questions to ask Why she was not hesitant is talking about that guy with her family?????????? Why the person, who loved me, hid the relation from everyone even from her close friends or simply she had played with my emotions????????????????????????? Is love related to physical aspect of a person or is it related to emotions????????? Last but not the least:- If someone loves the person like me simply because of mercy, am I an object of pity??? ?????????????? Do the persons like me have no right to love???

?????????????????????????????????? ??????????

"How it all happened? How?" I asked her with tears. "Forget about her dear. She does not deserve you, you will find a much better life partner, forget about her once and for all". "I am in tears Sonam. How can I forget her with whom I have spent two years of my life? Why she has done this to me?" I asked with a broken heart. "Leave her now dear, think about your life in future. I am feeling guilty, I should not have told you about her", she said with guilt in her heart. "Ok dear, I have to go now as I am not feeling well tonight, bye" I said. She replied, "Take care of yourself and close this chapter once and for all dear and please don"t lose heart, take care, God bless you". It was the most despairing moment of my life, even worst than the worst I have ever experienced. Even worse than my breakup day. I was in tears, was sleepless the whole night as if someone has taken something very precious away from me which is even more precious than my life. I kept thinking of the past, the moments spent with her. I was unable to understand what to do. I was like a dead person whose soul is out of his body. Sometimes thought of ending life, but destiny desired something else. "You have to live, not for yourself but for her, you have to. You have to find her wherever she is and with whom she is, ask her many questions, ask her that why she had ruined my life. Now, you have to ruin her life as she had done with you. 4 Part her from her husband, then she would be yours, wake up, wake up, you have to do that, you have to get your love at any cost, after all everything is fair in love and war", devil in me kept on telling me to do that. Next day was quite disturbing for me. I had a talk with my close friends. They tried to soothe my mind and I felt a little better but not so much. It was the mid of April, generally the marriage season and my beloved was also going to be married in the month. I didn"t know the exact date but whenever i saw a marriage ceremony it hurt me as I was reminded that my beloved was also going to be someone else"s. It really hurt me and brought tears into my eyes. The ghost of April 2009 haunted me very much. It seemed a gift which had been gifted to me by God, is going to be someone else"s now. Whenever I saw a newlywed couple, I was reminded of her which greatly disturbed my mind. I was in dismaying state. Often her remembrance haunted me. Her sweet voice, her beautiful smile, her love for me, her promises with me, the dreams we had seen together, dreamt of having a beautiful hut in the hill station, me and my beloved living a beautiful life where only love prevails, she in my arms and I having an infinite love for her, but all my dreams dashed to the ground. My love was in the mortuary and I was collecting the corpse of the time spent with her.

****

CHAPTER THREE

SOME SCRAPS OF MY COLLEGE DAYS

Some scraps of my college days Contentment is a great virtue, though it may not attract one's attention at first. Those who are truly content are usually quiet about it. It is a pleasure to be in their company, because they are full, peaceful, and generous. In my college days, I was a very introvert guy, didn"t talk much with girls. But I like to share my views through my poetries and writings for which sometimes I have to face criticism from my close ones. Big desires, big thoughts and big sayings all are the part of my life but more hypothetical than realistic, veil my emotions, my thoughts from everyone except me. In my college days I had a strong desire to be in love and be loved. In my graduation days I was infatuated for a girl living near my house. It was one sided love affair, she used to take tuitions with me in my school days and I never expressed what I felt for her as I myself didn"t know what was that. My heartbeat used to increase on seeing her. She used to come to my house to take books and notes from me. But I didn"t talk much with her. She was junior to me in my college. It was my strong desire to see her once a day. One day she left my college as she was going to join a course with some foreign university. I was very much hurt on hearing that. Though she didn"t know about my feelings for her yet I experienced the feeling of love for the first time in my life. Love is a very unique feeling and if it is both sided then nothing is sweeter than that. It is said that the spaces between our fingers were created so that another's could fill them in. It definitely changed my life and gave me a new enthusiasm and energy to live life and I thanked God for letting me experience this beautiful thing in life.

CHAPTER FOUR

STEP OF A LOVE IN MY LIFE

LOVE: We think about it, Sing about it, Dream about it && Loose sleep worrying about it. When we don't know we have it, we search for it. When we discover it, we don't know what to do with it. When we have it, we fear loosing it. It is the constant source of pleasure and pain. But we don't know which it will be from one moment to the next. It is a short word, easy to spell, difficult to define && IMPOSSIBLE to live without. "Love is a better teacher than duty." - Albert Einstein It was the mid of February 2006, I was standing with my friend Sunil on my roof top. I had completed graduation in engineering and used to help my brother in his business. Wanted to fly in sky, had high aims but my health seemed to be a big deterrence in that. Me and Sunil used to talk about everything, politics, new trends and girls etc etc etc etc. I was having a look on the contact list in his mobile and one number that struck was of a girl named Sonia. I asked him who the girl was. He told me that she was his classmate and now worked in airlines and also that it was very difficult to handle her. Being little bit overconfident I told him that nothing is impossible. Next day I sent her a message on her mobile phone "Hi. How are you?" She called and asked "May I know who you are?" I got confused and asked "Are you Maya?", then simply kept the phone. Maya being the name of my best friend in college struck to me in haste. I again send a message "Hi, I am Sunil"s friend, Can we be friends?" She asked "Which Sunil?" I replied "Your classmate in Masters" She replied "ok" Then I again asked her "Can we be friends?" She replied "Yeah, as you are Sunil"s friend, I am automatically your friend" 7 I was very happy and excited that day. It was mine first experience of a different type of friendship with a girl whom I had never seen. Being physically not fit I had always desired to be in company of a girl with whom I would have shared a special relationship like any other normal boy of my age. It is the stigma of Indian society that a person with any sort of disability is not accepted by a normal person of the opposite sex as a life partner or as a special friend. But I was very much excited about the girl without worrying about the impact of my disease on our relationship. Next day I sent her message "Hi, how are you, how was the day for you?" She replied instantaneously "Good, I am fine. What about you?" I replied "I am also fine. Do you have any boyfriend?" She replied "I am not that type of girl, so don"t ever think like that." It made me laugh as every girl would say the same and was not at all surprised. At that stage of life I was very hard hearted man, without love for anyone and not much for my family even. I only thought of my own pleasures, at whatever cost it may be. I had no idea that life was going to change and which would make me so soft hearted. So I started interacting with Sonia very frequently but only through messages on phone as I was too scared of talking to her directly and meeting also because I felt that if we meet then she would have come to know about my physical condition. She messaged me at 10 PM and asked "Where are you?" I replied "I was busy finding job for me on internet" She replied "Talk to me dear" I asked "So, what do you think about me?" She replied "You are a friend with whom I can share anything anytime and who will be there by my side whenever I need" This touched my heart and I am unable to express my feelings at that moment. I didn"t know what had happened to me that night, I was so happy without knowing reason for the same. Everything seemed so so beautiful. Life after that seemed so exciting and beautiful that I did not worry about my health condition and consequences of the same. We used to chat through messages on mobile phone for one month and I didn"t know even how her voice sounded. I was hesitant in talking to her and I think she also felt the same. 8 One day my friend Rohit asked me if there was someone who could tell about the fare of airlines as he had to go to Bangalore for interview. I said, "yes, one of my friends is in airlines" and I called her. I said "Hi" She had not expected my call. So hesitantly she replied "hi" I asked "one of my friends has to go to Bangalore, so can you please tell me the fare" She replied in a low tone "yeah, I will let you know tomorrow". I replied "ok". It was a strange experience of talking to a girl with whom I had good friendship but only through messages. Through messages we came to know well about each other. We cared for each other but on voice call it seemed as if we were strangers to each other. Next day she called me up and told about fares of airlines and asked me to repeat what she was told by her. I replied hesitantly but was not in order. She gave a laugh and cut the call. It was a great experience that she shared her laugh with me. I messaged her "your laugh is very beautiful". She replied "Thanks but I was very much scared while talking to you, don"t know why" I replied "Me too, and that"s why I didn"t remember what was said by you." Then next day I called her and talked to her. Now I was bit less hesitant in talking to her. I was feeling some energy in my body. I didn"t know from where it came. I felt as if some angel had stepped into my life and gave some meaning and strength to it. That night she called me at 1AM. I was very much surprised on getting call. We talked till 5 in morning. She asked me about my family etc etc. I asked her to cut the call but she kept on telling that she was not feeling sleepy and wanted to talk to me. That day I realised that Sonia had something for me and she really cared for me. But I could not gather courage to tell her about my health and about my inabilities. I was scared of telling her these things as I was afraid losing her. For the first time I blamed God and medical science for my sufferings. 9 It was my biggest mistake that I did not tell her the reality. Though I was getting the care and love of a girl, which I had never ever experienced in my life, but sometimes I felt that I was playing with her feelings. A thought was also there in my mind that true love never cares about anything or it does not have any condition. Sometimes I used to ask myself whether it is possible for a person to love another without even seeing her or him. Is this the love? Love with the voice only. But whatever I felt for her cannot be explained in words, then what was it? No one has defined love. Love is not the terminology but a feeling for someone, for whom you care. So I was experiencing new excitement in my life, we used to talk once during the day time and once at night, after dinner. I got selected in one of the competitive examination for the entry in a post graduation course. I called her "hi dear, I got selected in competitive exam for PG course" She replied "congrats, I have full faith in your abilities" But she said in a sad mood "now as you are going out of city, will you forget me?" I replied "No dear. How could I forget my dearest friend and it is because of you that I passed the examination" It seems strange that I gave the whole credit and not my family who were the main contributors. But love is a strange thing and I was also expressing my selfish nature. So a strong bond of friendship was getting formed between both of us. However there was an insecurity in my mind that whenever she comes to know the reality about me then what would happen to this so called love. Though we had feelings for each other but we had never ever expressed that. Feelings are to be expressed by deeds but not by words. My attitude changed for my family also. Now, I was more polite, started caring for my family, my mother. These changes were there in me because of that girl and it is truly said that "Behind every successful man there is a woman and behind every unsuccessful man also, there is a woman". May be I am getting too harsh for women, blaming them for everything. One incident which made me realize that it is impossible for me to live without her was that she was going to Bangalore for a training session of 7 days. 10 She called and said "you know I am going to Bangalore for a training session of seven days". I replied in a low tone "good". She asked "why you seem to be low?" I said, „nothing" She insisted then I said, "You will forget me and will find new friends there" She replied "I will not ever talk to you, good bye once and for all" I asked , "What happened dear? I am sorry if I hurt you, please never do this to me, I am sorry". She kept mum for few minutes. I was feeling as if someone had taken my heart out of my body. Then after the pause she spoke and I felt new energy in my body. These few minutes seemed so long. I astonished, what was happening to me and my emotions. She replied "Ok, that"s fine but don"t ever think so as I am your friend and will remain forever". I had a sigh of relief and I wondered that whatever is happening to me is good or bad, but it seemed a very beautiful thing without worrying about the consequences. While leaving for Bangalore she gave me a call from the airport. Her mother and a friend were accompanying her to see off her. She called and said, "Hello, how are you?" I replied, "Good. What about you?" She said, "I am leaving for Bangalore" I replied, "Good luck for your journey, take care of yourself." She gave a beautiful laugh and said, "You are saying the same thing which my mother said few minutes ago" I said, "I care for you like your mother". She replied with a sigh "I know" Then her mother came and she put the call on hold and had a word with her mother. After a pause she murmured, "Don"t cut the call, I want to talk to you till I board the plane" 11 She seemed low and said with tears in her eyes, "I am missing my father very much, if he would have been in this world, he would have been very happy for me." I said, "Don"t worry dear. His blessings would always be with you. I would always remain with you and give you strength". She said, "Let"s see, what happens. God has never been kind to me, and this time it should not be repeated, I pray to God. Ok, take care of yourself. I will try to call you whenever I get time. I am about to board the plane, if something happens to plane or me then you can remember me with these words, good bye" and cut the call. I was in tears and was unable to stop. I didn"t know what had happened to me that day; I keep on weeping without any reason. I was feeling so much emotional. Sonia lost her father few years back because of illness; she was the youngest of three sisters and loved by her father most. After her father"s death she missed him very much but never expressed this thing to anybody except me. This again showed that she also loved me as a special friend. She had to reach Bangalore via Delhi. On reaching Delhi she called me, "Hi, how are you? I am in Delhi airport waiting for the flight to take off for Bangalore." I replied, "Good, take care of yourself and take something to eat" She said, "Don"t worry, I will take care" I said, "I don"t know what has happened to me today, I am in tears without any reason." She sighed and replied, "Don"t worry. I am fine and safe here and good bye for now as I have to call my mother, bye, take care". I wondered if she knows the reason which I am unable to understand. Then she cut the call. I wanted to understand what she said but how could I understand other person"s feelings. That night there was no electricity due to rainy and stormy weather so I was in bed at 10"o clock. Now, I was very happy after talking to Sonia. I used to keep my mobile phone in cupboard. At around 11, I heard my mobile ringing but as I was sharing 12 the room with rest of my family, I could not gather courage to take the call. It rang for seven or eight times. I was sure it was Sonia. That night I was unable to sleep and was feeling sorry for her. She needed me and I was not available at that moment. Next day, I woke up early in morning and saw my mobile phone. There were eight missed calls, by three different numbers but surely it was not the number of my state. So I concluded that these were her calls from Bangalore. I waited eagerly for her call that day. The phone bell rang nearly at 2PM; it was her call as expected. She asked, "Where were you yesterday night? Do you know I called you from three numbers as I was feeling scared and lonely here, where were you?" I got emotional and replied, "Dear, I am so very sorry for that, I also had a sleepless night. It was difficult for me to take the call as my whole family was with me at that time. But I am feeling guilty that you needed me at that time and I was not available, I really care for you". She said, "It"s ok, I will talk to you at night, I have a class now and have to talk to mother also, take care, bye". I replied satisfactorily "Bye, you too take care of yourself" and she cut the call. At night she called me at 10:30 from the hotel room. That night I was ready to share with her something which I had never before. She said, "Hi how are you dear?" I replied "Good and what about you? Have you taken your dinner?" She said, "Yeah and you?" I replied "You forget me, first take care of yourself, I am at home and you are away" She said, "Ok, ok, I am not a child, I am grown up" She said these words in such a childish way that it touched my heart. Then we talked about her work and all. Suddenly she asked me something which stunned me and I took a pause for sometime. She asked, "You are talking to me now, but if I get married then with whom you will talk?" 13 I got stunned with these words and replied in low tone "I don"t know" I was in a deep thought and then she again asked, "Tell me, will you find someone else like me?" I replied in anger, "Shut up, I don"t know" Then after a brief pause I continued "I want to share something with you" She asked "what?" I said "I think, I have something in my mind for you, and I mean it" She sighed and replied "You think so but not sure" I said, "No, I am sure, I have feelings for you." She kept quite for sometime and then replied, "But I am not sure. God has taken all those things away from me which I loved. I lost my father whom I loved the most and if I say yes to you and unfortunately something adverse happens then I will not be able to bear it, I will certainly die" I said "I will not forget you ever, trust me" She replied, "You take your own time and try to understand what you have said today, If something happens to our relationship then I will not be able forgive myself for the rest of my life. I do not understand why God is so kind to me this time; he has taken all my beloved ones away from me. I don"t trust my destiny now. You also said that you think you have feelings for me but not sure. First you make sure that you mean whatever you have said. Try to give a thought to what I said. Bye, take care" She cut the call and I was silent for sometime thinking what she said. That night was again sleepless for me. I kept on thinking about her words and her fear of losing the things she loved.

Certainly, she was not rejecting my feelings for her but she wanted to warn me about any adverse consequences. But in the back of my mind a thought was there that how could I propose a girl, express my feelings for her without telling her the reality about my health condition. It was very unfair on my part as I was thinking only about my feelings and was playing with her feelings. She had every right to know about me. I was in great dilemma, whether to tell her the truth or not, but was of course afraid of losing her because she 14 would not have accepted me on knowing the reality. For the first time I was getting the romantic love of a girl and didn‟t want to lose that, so I decided not to tell the reality of my health to her. Though there was guilt at the small corner of my heart yet my selfishness overpowered my guilt. Till now we had not seen each other, it seems strange but that‟s true. This beautiful story makes this saying incorrect "love moves from eyes to heart". But in my case love started from heart and then move to eyes". To love someone is a wonderful feeling and persons who have never been in love in life have missed this beautiful experience. Love cannot be explained in words, it‟s only a feeling. I do not find the words to describe it. Now let‟s get back to my life. Next day was not like other days for me, I was thinking about my conversation with Sonia last night. I was also feeling insecure whether Sonia would call me today or not. But finally she called me at 11PM at and asked, "Hi, how are you dear?" I replied "I am all right; you tell, have you taken your meals?" She said "Don‟t worry, I am taking care of myself well" I said, "Forget whatever I told you yesterday, it was my feeling. I am so sorry if I hurt you with that conversation" She took a long breathe and said "Don"t be sorry, you told about your feelings and whatever I feel I told you" Then with a good bye she cut the call. I was feeling as if she was trying to say something but not able to express that thing. Feelings are to be felt but not expressed. How could I know what was there in her mind unless she expressed. Next day I learnt about one of her qualities which every traditional Indian girl must have. She called me at 11PM and asked, "How are you dear?" I replied "Fine dear, so how was the day?" She said "forget about that, I want to tell you something" I asked "what?" 15 She replied "Last night one of the girls was out of hotel for the whole night to be with her boyfriend". I said "Then what? It is her life. Why you are worried about these things?" She replied "I am not worried but this is not right before marriage and why are you supporting the girl who is doing wrong. I think you are also like her. You may also have relations before marriage, that"s why you are saying so". I said "I am not supporting but let her do what she wants to" She asked angrily, "How many girlfriends you have?" I replied "None but I may have one very shortly" She understood what I wanted to say and said after a brief pause, "I have to go to sleep now, take care, bye". It made me understand that she was like other traditional Indian women and she valued the Indian culture. But I was amazed why she was asking about my relationships. Perhaps she was getting possessive for me. Next day she had to come back to Jammu so I was eagerly waiting for her call. At 3PM I got a missed call from her but when I called back the number was not reachable. I was surprised.

She called me at 3:15PM from airport and said "Hi, I have reached safely in Jammu dear, I am back home". I replied, "Good to hear that but why did you gave a miss call me at 3PM?". She said "No dear! how could I? I was in plane at that time." I again asked her "No dear, check your call registry". She checked it and got surprised on seeing that there was a call from her mobile to mine at 3PM. She said, "How it could be possible dear as I have not called, but call registry shows that call was done, how it could be!" I replied "May be God wants me to be the first person with whom you talk on reaching Jammu". She replied with a long breathe, "I don"t know what God wants but he is not so generous to me ever then why this time" and said "good bye, talk to you at night, take care". 16 This incident made me believe that there was some supernatural power which was trying to bring us closer. But supernatural powers in 21st century, it"s unbelievable and moreover I did not have any faith in God. But then I thought maybe it is because of Sonia"s deep faith in existence of God. I was unable to understand and no technical person would ever understand that. But one thing I was feeling that I was going to be the most important person in her life. It reminded me of the saying that if you truly love someone then whole of the universe would try hardest to make sure that you get that love. But no one knows the destiny. Whole of the universe seems to be beautiful. I am up in the sky. Love is a very beautiful thing and whole world seems beautiful to the person who is in love. Even my family noticed the changes in me. My attitude for every one changed. Now I was more caring for my family. I started taking care of my mother. It seemed that I had learnt to love not only Sonia but my family also. There had always been a loving person hidden in me but it was Sonia who brought that love into my life. It was the first week of June. 6ᵗʰ June is my birthday and on 5ᵗʰ of June she called me at around 8 in evening. She said, "Happy birthday dear, I want to give you a present I am unable to gather the courage to face you, so I shall give it to your friend Sunil. Ask him to meet me in university" I replied "Ok, I would ask him" At sharp 12 in night she called, "Hi, happy birthday dear, many many happy returns of the day. May god bless you." I replied "thanks dear and I pray to god that I can celebrate all my birthdays with you" She took a long breathe and cut the call. I did not insist on meeting her as I was scared of loosing her. But I didn"t understand why she hesitated to give the gift personally to me. Next day she took half day leave from her 17 office to meet Sunil so as to give him the gift. But due to some reason Sunil could not be at university. She called me in the evening. She said sadly, "Your friend did not meet me. I waited him for two hours, I had taken leave also. Where was he?" I replied, "Dear I don"t know the reason, but may I know what was the gift for me" She said "Chocolates, but now I will have to eat all that. My mother asked me about all these chocolates but I lied, it"s too bad" I replied with smile "You ate or I ate it"s the same thing so don"t worry dear. Don"t feel guilty for that" Again thought came in my mind whether I was doing right or not. I was in a fix but I decided to let the things go on. With time I was getting closer to her and same for here. One day I called her and asked, "How are you janu?" She replied, "Janu! What"s that?" I said "It"s the name given to you by me" She said in a childish tone "Ok as you wish" After that I frequently used the words "janu" and "my sonia" and she never objected to that, rather she loved to hear those words. One day I messaged her at night "Sonia, I love you. It"s impossible for me to live without you. Do you love me? If you have same feelings for me then give me a miss call before 10 in morning". Next day I was waiting for her miss call since 6 in the morning. I was waiting as if I was getting some reward or waiting for the result of an examination. There were mixed emotions in my mind. I was thinking if she says "no" then what will happen. It seemed to be a matter of life and death for me. Minutes seemed to be as long as days or years .I was very much nervous. Now its 9:55AM, I was getting negative thoughts. But suddenly 18 everything changed. I got a call at 9:59AM, it was her call and everything changed after that. I was feeling as if I have got everything I have ever desired for in life. I thanked God for being so kind to me. I was really unable to believe that the person whom I loved the most also loved me. It was perhaps one of the most important moments of my life. Then I tried to tell her about my health. I messaged her that there is problem in my muscles and I have difficulty in walking. She called me and said very coolly, "You should take the ashvagandha with milk to cure the weakness in your legs. I will give it to your friend Sunil tomorrow. You should take that and you will be all right." I replied "Ok dear, I will purchase it myself. Tell me from where I can get that" She told the place and brand (which was owned by a particular saint whom I didn"t trust at all). But I agreed. Just because she had asked me I started trusting the saint also. Earlier I even used to exchange words with my mother over his truthfulness. But love made me believe that saint also. Even a lie seems to be the truth when spoken by beloved ones. That is the power of love. Next day she asked me about ashvagandha. I lied that I had consulted my doctor in Amritsar (where my treatment had been going on) and he suggested me not to take that. She trusted me. I thought I might lose her love if I told her more than that. So I thought that with time she would get apprised of my actual condition. Now it was the time to go for the interview for the higher studies. She seemed to be little sad. She called me on the day I was leaving and said "Hi Sameer" I replied, "Hi janu, I am leaving for interview along with my brother, pray to God that I am successful in it" In a happy but little sad tone she said, "Yeah, I always pray for you dear. Wish happy and safe journey." It reminded me of the basic nature of a woman, that is, to be always so loving and caring. Truly I was touched by these words. I said, "You take care of yourself". 19 She replied, "You also take care, take food properly and don"t forget to message me after every one hour during journey otherwise I will not talk to you". She was getting too emotional. It really brought tears in my eyes. She was getting possessive for me and I was feeling so much love for her that it"s impossible to explain. Next day I left for that place. Before leaving I called her to say good bye. I messaged her frequently. My interview was scheduled for next day; we (me and my brother) stayed at my friend"s place. We reached at 7PM in the evening. My brother and friend went out and I decided to remain at home only. I called her and said "Hi janu, how are you?" She replied "I am fine. How are you, have you reached safely there, have you taken lunch, tea etc. etc. etc. etc.?" she asked so many questions without taking break. I replied "I am fine dear. I know you care for me a lot. I am taking care of myself well so don"t worry" She said "If you don"t take care of yourself then I will not talk to you. My mom is coming so bye and take care" I said "Bye. God bless you" I got emotion and messaged to her, "Sonia I love you very much, more than anything else in life, just be with me for the whole life. It is unable to live without you now. I will take care of you well. I will take care of our children. I love you very much and I know that you also love me very much but it is difficult for you to express being a girl. But I love you and don"t ever think of leaving me." In love a person doesn"t understand what he is saying. He is in love and whole world seems to be lovable to him. I made all imaginations about our marriage and life after that. It seems strange but when the person is in love then he can imagine anything he likes no matter whether it is practically possible or not. Next day I got up early in the morning and called her before leaving for interview. Her mother picked up the phone and said "Hello, hello, who are you? With whom do you want to talk?" I didn"t respond and disconnected the call. Her 20 mother seemed to be angry because of the call. But I had to go for interview, so I left. I got selected in the interview and at noon I called her, "Hi janu, I got selected in interview" She said in an emotional tone "Congrats for that, now you will have to leave Jammu" I replied, "Don"t worry dear; I am always with you, my soul remains with you only." She said "Let„s see. Have you taken lunch? If not then cut the call and take lunch now" I replied "Ok, ok dear, I know you care for" Then she said "You called in the morning, my mother asked me many questions related to the call .Now go and take lunch and call me when you reach home." I replied "Ok dear, you are so lucky for me. I got selected in it because of your wishes." It shows how an Indian girl has to make adjustments due to the restrictions imposed on her by her parents or elders but she is ready to adjust with these restrictions with for her love and that is true in my case also. It once again shows my selfish nature, everything was being done by my family and I was giving credit to that girl. But at that time I was in love and far away from reality. But that"s love. In love a person thinks about his lover and nothing else. On the journey back to Jammu, I listened the song of a recently released movie „Krish" (A Bollywood movie) starring Hrithik Roshan and Priyanka Chopra many times and imagined that I was singing it for her. Dhup niklti hai jahan se, chandni behti hai yahan tak Khabar ye ayi hai wahan se, koi tumsa nahin, koi tumsa nahin On reaching Jammu I gave her a miss call at 12 midnight to inform that I had reached home safely and in return she also gave a miss call. I felt that she was eagerly waiting for me to reach Jammu and was awake till that time. 21 I had to leave Jammu after a week. So these days were crucial for me. I had to make preparations for going. She seemed to be little sad may be as I was leaving. Still we had never seen each other, strange but true. Now I believed that the true love is between two persons irrespective of their physical appearances. But it was far away from reality. However sometimes I felt insecure also that if I met her personally then what would be her reaction on seeing me. Did she truly love me or she loved me just because I was well educated and belonged to a good family. I did not have the strength to tell her the truth. I decided to let the things go on like that only and let time decide the fate of our relation. Now it was the time to leave Jammu. I had to leave next day morning. I packed all the things required. In evening she called me and said with emotions, "Hi, how are you? So, you are leaving tomorrow, take care of yourself well and call me daily. Don"t forget me." I replied, "How can I forget myself dear? You are my soul and thus you always remain with me." She said with a long breathe, "What if you find someone else there and forget me?" I replied angrily, "Shut up, you are my love and I love you more than anything else." Then I asked her to put the call on hold and to listen the song (A bollywood song). Tum ko bhi hai khabar, Mujhko bhi hai pta Ho raha hai judaa, Dono ka raasta, Dur jaake bhi mujhse tum meri yaadon main rehna Kabhi alvida na kehna, Kabhi alvida na kehna. We talked for around two hours. She was feeling very emotional and sad on my departure. Next morning I left Jammu. It was a new beginning for me. On the way I messaged her many times. I was so much lost in her love that I even forgot my mother. Now I feel guilty but I didn"t know what had happened to me that she was had become the most important person in my life and all others were secondary. It was a great mistake on my part. 22 Next day I was in my hostel. I called her in the evening and had a talk with her. Here there were no barriers as none could listen to our conversation and I could talk freely without any hesitation.

CHAPTER FIVE

ATTITUDE CHANGE

"Attitude is a little thing that makes a big difference." - Winston Churchil The first day at college was quite an exciting one, new place, new friends, new girls but my love remained the same as I loved her by heart. I used to talk to her after my lunch and she insisted on not talking too long as call charges were quite high and I might feel burdened being a student. About fifteen days had passed since I left Jammu. Then one day phone network was not working, I kept on trying to call her but was unable to call her at my fixed time that is after lunch. But I was receiving her messages. I received message, "Where are you dear?" I tried to call her back but it was not working. It was the same till evening. At 7 in the evening I called her from a PCO booth. She got emotional on hearing my voice and asked me in great desperation, "Where were you? Do you know how much I am concerned about you? I was praying for you to be all right. I was in a fix what to do, how to contact you. Do you know how much I ....". After these words she was quiet for sometime. I was touched by these words. There were tears in my eyes; I felt her intense love for me. I replied, "Don"t worry dear, I am all right. I know you care for me. But network was working properly here, that is why I could not call." She said "Ok, no worries. Take care of yourself." I was feeling bad for her. She cared so much for me and I had concealed such a big fact about me from her. One day I met a guy from Jammu, Anil whose sister was Sonia"s colleague. He was my batch mate here. Sonia told her about me. The first impression I got about him was that he was a cunning and selfish but later on I realized that he was a practical and experienced guy who had gone through all phases of life. Soon he became a good friend of mine. Sonia often talked of his sister"s strict nature. Once she called me and said, "Do you know what"s your friends sister has done? Fatty girl!!" I replied in a low tone as I was also fatty, "What?" 24 "She interferes in all of my matters; I will not tolerate this thing. Give me the phone number of her mother. I will ask her what she had taught to her daughter", She said angrily. I replied "Dear don"t be so aggressive. Why will you talk to her mother? Dear official matters should be dealt with in office only. She might me right in her place. I do not like this on your part. Whenever you are angry just hold your fingers tight and your anger will vanish" She took a sigh of relief and said "I think you are right and I was overreacting, but if somebody does wrong to me I will not forgive him or her, whether it is she or you". She said angrily. These words scared me a little bit and I thought what would happen to me when she would come to know about the reality. That day I came to know about her aggressive nature and disliking for fat people. I was feeling insecure as I was also fatty. Her aggressive nature was also a cause of concern to me. It"s strange that a person who himself was aggressive, wanted to make efforts to reduce the aggressiveness of other person. But I was no longer aggressive. It all changed when she came into my life. A person goes through lot of changes when he or she is in love and I was also experiencing the same. It went on like this. She trusted me and I did not have the courage to tell her the truth. One day I messaged her "Dear it is becoming difficult to live without you now. What can be done?" She replied "What can we do? It can be done by our families only". I messaged her again "But I want to share something with you and which is very important." She asked, "What!" I replied, "Dear I have muscle related problem and treatment is going on." She took a long pause and I messaged her again, "What happened dear?" She messaged after a few minutes, "What can I say? I am very much worried on hearing that, I don"t know what to say". I again messaged her, "Dear, do you love me?" 25 She replied, "I don"t express my feelings but I have feelings for you and that"s why I am very much worried" I messaged her again, "Have your feeling changed on knowing that about me?" She replied, "I have feelings for you and it will always remain. If my feeling change then God will punish me" I was shocked on hearing that. I once again realized how much she loved me. I replied back "Don"t say such things dear". At that time I was in abysmal love which cannot be explained in words. I don"t find the words to explain it. I thought about her only and nothing else in the world. I felt that the love is not with physical aspect of a person but it is with the soul, and it was true in my case as we had never seen each other but we had abysmal love and care for each other. I started respecting her even more. One day she called and said, "I am very much afraid today". I asked, "What has happened dear?" She replied in a low tone, "There is a proposal for my marriage; he is a subinspector in police". I was shocked and asked desperately "What will happen now?" She said, "My mother is forcing me to marry that guy" I asked "What have you decided?" She replied "I will out rightly reject that proposal. Let"s see what happens in the evening". I was quiet upset on hearing that. I didn"t know what to do and what to say. She called me in evening and said, "You know, I was praying to God for whole day that my mother rejects that proposal otherwise it will not be good for you and me". I wanted to cry. I was thinking if something adverse would happen, then what? I tried hard to hide my feelings but she felt my anxiety and told me not to worry. That night was sleepless for me. I was worried and felt as if someone was taking something, which was very dear to me away from me. It was unbearable. That night seemed to be as long as years. I was in abysmal pain which is difficult to describe through words. People often 26 say that in love you have to bear the pain, which I was experiencing for the first time in my life. I questioned myself that why it always happened to me Next day I called her, "Dear, what your mother has decided?" She replied "Last evening I told my mother that I will marry a police personnel, I don"t like them. She was very angry over that but she cooled down later on. I remained disturbed and kept on thinking what to say to my mother but somehow I managed that. Everything would be all right. After all I have to decide for my future and I know better what is good for both of us".

I took a sigh of relief and said, "Ok dear, thanks for trusting my love" Now I was sure that she would do anything for my love. This strange love story went on and with time I became more possessive for her. In an Indian society, a girl is subjected to so many restrictions which a boy doesn"t have. She was not allowed to go out in late hours and whenever she had to go somewhere, she had to give explanation for that. If she talked to someone on phone, had to give the whole explanation about the person with whom she was talking. This shows the disparity in our society which is still there. My possessiveness for her increased and whenever she couldn"t take my call, so many questions would arise in my mind that where she was, with whom etc etc. One day I called her when she was at home. It was Saturday, she was with her relatives. She did not take the call. I tried nearly for 20 times. Finally she took the call told me about the presence of relatives at home. I insisted on her to talk to me. But she refused. I message her, "Dear I am feeling very tired today, something is happening to me I don"t know what it is". She didn"t respond to that. Then I concocted a story so as to make her feel that she had done a wrong thing by not answering my call. I wanted to make her feel that. It was not fair on my part but I did that. I messaged her late in night, "My heart is paining very much I don"t know why?" I did send the same message three or four times and then stopped sending messages. Next day my plan went on as I had desired. She called me from office five to six times but I didn"t respond. Then she called from two other phone numbers but I didn"t respond as I knew that these were her calls only. I wanted her to be worried about me. 27 In the evening I messaged her, as I thought that was enough for her, "Dear, I was in hospital last night. Something happened to me and my friends took me to hospital. My heart was paining very much". She didn"t respond to that. I realized that I had done wrong, she loved me so much and I had been making stories to hurt. I called her so many times but she didn"t answer. The next week was very painful for me, as she didn"t attend any of my calls and I thought I deserved that. I had done wrong to her. It was too heartening for me as I had never been ignored like this by her. Not a single day had gone without talking to her since I met her. I met her in February and it was October now. But how selfish and cunning I was, as I hurt her by concocting a story of pain in my heart. I didn"t realize at that time that a girl was bound by so many restrictions at home and she had to abide by them. I was in love with her but I didn"t know what to do as she was not answering my calls. I was so sad those days and used to cry loud at night. Talking to her was a part of my daily routine, like eating and breathing. I felt as if there was a void in my life. After a week she responded to my call and said, "Listen Sameer, I don"t want to talk to you" I asked, "Why dear?" She said, "I have some family compulslons" I said, "I am sorry if I have hurt you, but please don"t do this to me" Then suddenly a story erupted in my cunning mind. I had heard that a girl was always jealous of other girls. I told her, "Dear, I met one of my dear friends, we were in same class at school, and she is now a dentist in Jammu, she was my best friend at school and we have very good family relations also." The trick worked, she asked in a low tone, "Where was she for all these years?" I replied, "Her father was in army and now he has retired. Now, they have settled permanently in Jammu. I got her contact number and we talk daily. When we were in school we were best friends and my friends often thought that there was a special relationship between both of us. They used to tease us by calling us as lovers, jodi, made for each other, some people were even sure of our marriage" 28 She took a pause and asked, "Do you call her daily now?" I replied, "No, I don"t, rather she calls me daily" In an emotional tone she asked, "Does she love you?" I replied, "May be, but she is only a good friend for me." She again asked, "Do you love her?" I replied angrily "Shut up, I love only one girl and that is you. Do you know how much I have cried during last week when you did not respond to my calls? Do you know how much I love you?" She replied, "I am so sorry but I was annoyed with you. Something has happened in my family also which I will tell you in evening". Then she cut the call. My trick worked, I was very happy over that. But there was a guilty feeling in a corner of my heart as I had lied to the girl who trusted me like anything. But at that time I was very desperate for her, I wanted her to be back in my life at whatever cost it may be. I knew that it was wrong on my part to concoct a story about a girl who never existed in my life but I was satisfied that I had lied for the sake of my love for her, after all it is said that everything is fair in love and war. She called me in evening, "Dear I was very angry with you" I replied, "I know I didn"t respond to your calls that day, but I was not in a good condition that day and had to go to hospital, my heart was paining very much. Doctor said that any delay in treatment would have been risky to my life". I lied with so much confidence that she had to believe that. She replied, "Oh, really?" I replied with confidence, "Yeah, I was thinking about you only. I wanted to share my pain with you, so I insisted on talking to you" She said, "Ok but I didn"t know that the situation was so grave. I was angry with you as you kept on calling me knowing the fact that there were relatives at my place. You must try to understand the limitations of a girl. Inspite of me feeling sorry you were angry and didn"t respond to my calls. I thought that you don"t understand me and my limitations". 29 Then I replied with confidence "Dear, try to understand me I was not well that night. I wanted to talk to you only and share my pain with you only. I did not tell my family about this". She said, "It"s not right; I know you trust me, but you should have told about it to your family. You should take care in future and promise me that it will never happen again". "Ok dear, I will and promise you that it will not happen again" I replied. "One more thing, last Sunday my uncle came to our place and scolded me for rejecting the marriage proposal of police personnel. He also tried to make me realize that I was doing wrong to my mother by rejecting that proposal. My mother was also badly hurt and was in tears. She wants me to marry soon so that she is able to fulfill all her responsibilities. She is left alone to take care of us after the death of my father. I thought that I have some duty towards my mother also, so I was trying to put an end to our relation" she said. I replied, "Dear, I will take care of you and your mother, your responsibility are mine also. I love you very much." She said, "I am also sorry for not attending your calls and neglecting you, I am sorry, sorry, sorry….." Ok dear, don"t be, I love you, I love you, I love you….." after saying that I was lost in her dreams and had a sound sleep that night, almost after a week. So my plan was successful and went as desired by me but I was feeling guilty for having lied to the girl who trusted me so much and believed in my words. It was my second lie. I kept on sending messages to her and called her daily. She had kept my messages hidden in her mobile and were locked with a security code. One day her sister asked her about the security code, but Sonia resisted giving that. On it her sister cursed her a lot and asked her mother to marry her off on the pretext that otherwise she might bring disrepute to their family. She told me about the whole episode. I advised her to delete all the messages sent by me. She said, "Why? I will not." I said in a serious tone, "Dear they will force you otherwise to get married very soon, which will not be good for both of us." 30 She replied in a childish tone, "Can I come to your place?" I said, "Why not dear? I love you." She asked, "Will your family accept me?" I said, "Dear ours is a very nice family, they will be very happy if you come to our place. Your sweet voice and laugh will make it a heaven." She replied, "My sister always keeps an eye on me. I don"t like that; I have my own life and if you are with me then what is the problem. Are you?" "Yeah dear, I love you and I will always be with you" I replied emotionally. One day she went to the place of her cousin"s fiancé. She had lunch there and called me after lunch. She said, "Dear I am at the place of my cousin"s fiancé. They all are forcing me to visit his friend"s place as they want me to marry him. He is in air force" I asked, "Will you go there?" She replied angrily, "Are you mad? I have taken the decision and no one can change my decision". "What you have decided?" I asked with a little smile. "You know better and if you do not stop asking such silly questions, I will not talk to you" she said. I laughed." Ok dear, I am joking. What did you say to your relatives" I asked her. She replied, "I simply said that I didn"t want to go there". I respected her for trusting me without even meeting me. Now I was sure about one thing that she really loved me and could go to any extent for me. But I was not sure if it was right or wrong on my part and felt that I was playing with her feelings but I was scared of losing my love. I was not sure how could she react on seeing me. But I had trust in my love. One day Sonia called me and said, "Dear, I am feeling guilty as it was not good on my part to conceal the truth from my family. My mother trusts me and I am hiding the truth from her, it is not right". "What can be done dear?" I asked her. 31 "I will tell my brother about you and he will meet you in December, Is it right? Can you meet him dear?" I replied hesitatingly, "Ok, as you wish". "I think it"s not right to hide our relation from the family, I am feeling very guilty." She said. "We love each other. If we are doing it for our good in long term then we are not at fault, I think. But if you want to tell this to your mother then it is ok" I said. "No, I will first talk to brother and then he will try to convince my mom" she replied. She did not have any real brother but she had a school friend whom she considered as her brother. "But what will I tell my brother, that we have never seen each other, isn"t it strange?" I asked, "So, what you have decided?" "I have decided to lie to my brother and say that we met in university. I know it is not right but how can I tell him that we love each other without even seeing each other." she said. "Ok, as you wish" I replied. "Ok. I will ask him to meet you in December because then you shall be here for your vacations, take care, bye dear" Then she cut the call. Now I was feeling very anxious and worried about her reaction when she would come to know of my health condition and now it was certain because she was going to ask her brother to meet me. It was sure that she would get hurt on knowing that as I had concealed this from her. I was thinking that she trusted me and I was playing with her feelings. Till now, I had been living in a hypothetical world, but now I realized the seriousness of our relation. But it was my nature to take everything easy, so I didn"t think much about it. I was convincing myself to let the things go on like that and not to worry about future repercussions. I was sure to handle the situation. However I asked many questions to myself: "How will she react on seeing me?" 32 "Is it right to hide the truth from her?" "Is it right to break the trust of a person who loves you so much?" "Does true love care about the looks and physical appearance of a person or is it simply a philosophy?" "Is it right to tell her the truth and lose my love or is it right to act as a traitor and conceal the truth?" "How will her brother react on seeing my condition?" "Does a person like me do not has the right to love someone?" "Is love is only for the able bodied persons and not for persons like me?" "Will she respect me anymore on seeing me?" Now, I was out of my virtual world in which I was living for the last ten months. This incident shook my emotions and forced me to think about the life without her, as I was sure that she would not be with me on seeing me. She was like any other normal girl in this world and not a unique one. That night was sleepless for me and for the first time I asked God that why He allows pain to His creatures and why He does not create able bodied persons only and why had He chosen me only to bear all this pain?. I was in tears due to not only the guilty feeling but as well as the fear of losing her. But I was also satisfied that at least someone loved me be it for few months only but I experienced the love. What is love? Everyone has one"s own interpretation of love. Some feel that it is nothing but simply infatuation; some others feel that it"s a fun; still others feel that it is an emotion. The left others feel that emotion plus sex is love. But how can a person interpret it without feeling it. My interpretation of love is in following lines: Love is the feeling which can never be explained but felt, it brings a person to a new height and at the same time give a person abysmal pain for which no antibiotic would be there, some people say that to posses your love may not be love but if you don't get your love you would also be a lover. But if you don't possess your love, then was it the true love? If you love something, let it go. If it comes back to you, it's yours forever. If it doesn't, then it was never meant to be. love for me is eternal feeling which can be diminished with death only, love can be done only once and rest is just life, that's true, 33 true love never fades, it will remain as young as a child, when you see your love, the glare of Taj Mahal would be less than that, it seems strange but that's true, everyone must taste love once and must be strong enough to bear the pain, its really heartening. In love person can learn many things from his beloved. The famous urdu poet Mirza Ghalib has rightly said about love: "Ye ishq nahin asan itna to samz lije, ek aag ka darya hai aur dub ke jana hai".

CHAPTER SIX

HER POSSESIVENESS FOR ME

"When you are in Love you can't fall asleep because reality is better than your dreams." Let"s move back to the story. The life was going on with a lot of excitement. Every day I was experiencing some thing new in love. One of her cousins was going to get married soon. She used to talk to her fiancé in the evening at every alternate day. It was the day of her cousin"s engagement ceremony. She called me in evening, "Hi dear, do you know I am with my cousin and today is her engagement ceremony." I replied, "Ok that"s good dear". She said amazingly, "Her fiancé is so smart, slim and handsome. I was astonished on seeing him". I asked, "Why dear?" She asked, "Are you also smart and handsome?" I replied in a low tone, "Yes dear." I was shocked. She was comparing me to her brother-in-law, that"s natural human tendency but how could I react to that. I was not at all slim. I was fatty. I was thinking that she had lots of expectations and what would happen the day she would meet me, whole of her expectations would dash to ground. But how could I tell her the truth. I was again in a dilemma what to do and what not to. She frequently used to tell me about her cousins fiancé. I could never react to that. One day when I called her, her cousin asked her that who had called, she told her that it was her friends call. So she was in the process of telling her family about me. It was the mid of November. She called me, "Who are you?" I replied, "I am Sonia"s Sameer" She said, "I am her sister, not Sonia, how do you know Sonia?" I replied "I love her and want to marry her." She asked "How did you meet her?" I replied "I love her, she was my friend"s friend, and we have not seen each other as yet." 35 But it was Sonia only. She said, "Don"t ever say this thing to my sister or any other member of my family. Tell them that we met in university. It seems strange that we love each other and have not seen each other as yet; everyone would make fun of our love. Whenever you happen to talk to my family, just tell them that we met in university. It"s a lie but we will have to do that so that our love is not laughed at." Generally in love two people meet each other and then fall in love but in our case it was totally different. We had never seen each other still we loved each other by heart and love each other"s voice. She used to talk to her cousin"s fiancé and discuss with me ever thing about her conversation with him and every time asked me a question, "Are you also like him?" Generally, the girls compare their boyfriends and husband to others" boyfriends or husbands. Whenever she found him wrong on any account she used to ask me whether I also do the same and if my answer was yes then she tried to make me amend the same. One day she called me and said "You know! My cousin is trying to call her fiancé for last few hours and his phone is busy for such a long time. What can be the reason? Any guesses?" "No dear, how could I?" I replied. "He might be having a girlfriend, so busy with talking to her. I will have to tell about it to my uncle so that he can reconsider about marriage" she said angrily. "No dear, he might be busy with some work. Don"t jump to any conclusion in haste as it may affect their relation." I said "Poor girl, she is in trap of that guy" she said angrily. "Why are you thinking negatively and you seem to be a very narrow minded girl" I said. "Oh, mind your language, you are also like him, you might also be having a girlfriend. If it really happens then I will kill you definitely" she cut the call angrily. I was stunned on hearing that, but also felt secured that she was possessive about me. Definitely she was little bit narrow minded. 36 I had also started drinking occasionally which was known just to my friends only. Next day I called her and said, "How you are dear and how is your cousin?" "She is fine. Yesterday you stopped me from doing a foolish thing, I am thankful to you, he was really busy in his office work that is why his phone was busy, Thank God, I did not do that otherwise no one could forgive me ever." She said with a sigh of relief. "You should always take suggestions from me." I replied with smile. "Ok. But tell me one thing, do you drink?" she asked with suspicion. "What? Are you mad? No one in my family drinks and none of the previous generations have ever." I replied angrily. "Ok, but you know my cousin"s fiancé drinks, so bad" she said. "Yeah, it is bad to drink" I said in a low tone. But the scene was totally different. I used to drink on weekends with my friends and I kept it secret from my family and from my beloved Sonia also. Thinks kept going on like that.

I used to make plans with her for our life after marriage. We frequently talked about that. Here I want to share something. It was my examination time in December, I was preparing for my examination next day. She gave me a miss call but I didn"t respond as I was busy. Then she called me and said, "Where were you? Forget me if you don"t want to talk to me". "No dear. Tomorrow is my examination so I was preparing for that" I replied. "But don"t forget me, I am also important to you" she said emotionally. "Ok dear. What"s going on? Have you taken dinner" I asked her. "Yeah, take care of yourself" she said "Ok, when I will be with you, you will take care of me" I said. "Ok, but I would stay at my mother"s place after marriage. I would marry you, if you agree to it" she said. "Ok dear. I will allow you to go to your mother"s place on weekends. So you can be with her for two days a week." I said. 37 "No, I will go for 3 days a week and daily after my office hours I will go to meet my mother first and then will come home. Is it ok?" She said with a cunning smile. "I agree, I will tell you everything after marriage" I replied. "You might change after marriage and will forget all this, it happens in every love marriage" she said. "Do not worry, I will keep my word." I replied. "But I feel scared on the thought that if our marriage does not happen then what will I do" she said emotionally and then she cut the call after saying bye to me. I also got little bit disturbed on hearing that, this thing literally haunted me. I knew the future of our relationship by my intuition. But I took it lightly and thought that whatever destined, would happen. If destiny is to be with her then we will get married, if not then I would get someone better than her. She was much concerned about me and my health. She asked me to do yoga daily and used to enquire about the time when I did that. I was not regular in doing it but I used to lie to her even if I had not done yoga. Here I would narrate one incident, which I think was the worst on my part. She called me at 8 in the evening, "Hi motu(fatty), how are you? I have called you to tell that baba Ramdev(yoga guru) is coming to Amritsar next week, you see him there and ask him about your health. Can you go?" I got little frustrated and replied, "Ok I will, if you insist". I wanted to show her that I was doing so many things for her. I wanted to make her so much emotional for me as I felt good in that. "Thank you dear. I will give you the phone number so that you can contact him. I hope you will get well and it would be the happiest thing for me in my life as I will get what I have desired for" she replied in an emotional tone. "Janu, don"t worry, everything would be all right. I will go there", I replied. Now it was the day when I once again lied to her. I told her that I had registered myself for yoga in Amritsar. On the day I was supposed to be in Amritsar, I did not take her calls as I had told her that I was in Amritsar for the yoga session. She called me so many times. I was in the hostel with my friend and he kept on asking me to pick the 38 phone. But I told him that it was of my girlfriend and I had lied to her that I was in Amritsar for a yoga camp, so I could not take the call. I would call her later to tell her that I was busy in yoga camp. After sometime I called her, she asked so many question to me, "Hi motu, where were you? Did you attend the camp? What did he say? "Yeah, I attended that and that"s why I could not take your call. It was a huge gathering there and babaji was not approachable. But I had a talk with his followers and they told me about a few exercises". I lied with confidence. "What they did they tell you? How much time will it take to cure? Have they prescribed any medicine? She asked "Yes dear, they told me about the exercise only. They told me that that I will get well if I exercise regularly" I said "Good, now I will instruct you when to do and how to do. I will watch it on TV and will let you know. I will call you in evening dear. May God bless you with good health, I daily pray to God for that. God has not been so kind to me but if this time it does not happen then I will never pray. Tell me one thing, you are in Amritsar but the noise in your background is the same as it is in your hostel. Are you really in Amritsar" She asked suspiciously. "Dear, I am in my friend"s hostel and all hostels are the same, that"s why you are hearing same type of noise. Do you trust me?" I lied with confidence. "Yeah dear I trust you." She cut the call in an emotional tone. I also got emotional as I was feeling that she cared so much for me and I lied to her so many times, especially about the matters concerned with my health. I was in tears but I was also helpless. I was going through a grave emotional phase, so was not able to tell her the truth. Now I felt a new energy in my body. I started doing yoga regularly. Though I lied to her yet felt that if Savitri could bring her husband"s soul back from Yamraj, then my problem not being that severe could also be cured with her prayers. I was feeling new energy and was optimistic that I would be alright. It went on like that for days. It was the month of December and we had vacations for few days so I was going home. 39 Usually we talked about our love but never ever thought of discussing anything related to physical relations. One day while talking to her I said "Kiss you dear muah". She cut the call. I called her back but she did not answer the call. When I kept on calling her again and again she finally took my call and said, "Listen, I don"t want to talk to you, you say such things, I don"t like this, I am not like other girls". I said sorry to her. I realized that she was a bit narrow minded but I still loved her more than anything else. She had a friend named Shivali who was working in the same office as her. I used to talk to her frequently. She used to address me as bhaiya and Sonia as bhabhi. I felt great on hearing that .It was December 2006 and my semester was over and we had vacations now. Before I left for Jammu she called me and said "Hi dear, I want a favor from you. Dear when Shivali"s boyfriend asked me about you I told him that you are studying masters in engineering, he was astonished that how could I have such an educated and intelligent guy as my boyfriend. He seems to be jealous of you and also asked me to show your photograph. Can you send your photograph to me? I want to show it to him so that they believe that you are my boyfriend. Please send it at the earliest to me" she said. I did not know how to react to that as I was fatty and she disliked fatty persons. So, I thought of an idea. I took my identity card and scanned it and search for the photoshop editor for editing my picture. Somehow I was successful in doing that. I cropped my photograph so as to look slim. It was not right on my part as I was again lying to her but I didn"t

want to lose her. I did send her that. Next day she called me and said, "What type of photograph have you sent to me? I don"t want to talk to you as everyone made fun of me at my office; I was very much ashamed of that". "Dear I don"t have any camera. As you were in hurry yesterday so I did send that only to you, but next time I will definitely send the proper photograph to you. Don"t worry dear", I replied. "You are a liar, I don"t want to talk to you, don"t talk to me", she replied angrily and put off the call. 40 I was feeling guilty as I had lied to her, made fun of her trust but she was everything to me and I never thought of my life without her. Days passed and now it was vacation time. She frequently called me on my way to Jammu. I was feeling good. I was at home in the evening. The first thing I did was to message her to tell that I had reached home safely. I enjoyed the meal cooked by my mother; I was eating it almost after six months. At around 8 in evening she gave a miss calls on my landline phone, for 5 or 6 times. My mother wondered that who was that crazy person but how could I tell her that this crazy person was everything to me and I have made her a part of my life. I talked to her after that and she said, "Listen, I will ask my brother to meet you in your next visit to Jammu so that decision about our marriage is taken." I was mute on hearing that as I was sure of losing her when anyone from her family or she would meet me. But still in some corner of my heart there was a faith in destiny and God that this time He would not be so unfair to me, if he existed somewhere in the universe.
****
****

CHAPTER SEVEN

FIRST METTING WITH MY LOVE

One day she called me in the morning and asked "Dear, come to your brother"s office as I am coming to the bank near that office. I have some work there and also want to see you". Now what could I do? I was thinking in heart of heart that true love never goes by physical aspect, so I went there in an ordinary dress only. At that time my dressing sense was very poor and also I had long hair. I never cared about my appearance. So I went there wearing a simple trouser and T-shirt. As per me I was looking good. She wanted to see me from a distance only. But she didn"t want me to see her, I didn"t know why. She called me when she was in front of the bank, "Where are you? Come out of office". My heartbeat increased and finally I came out. She again said, "I am not able to see you." I sat on a chair there and said, "I am right in front of you dear". "I am not able to see you, here is only a very fatty man sitting on chair. Waive your hand" she replied. I waived my hand and said, "I am waiving my hand and the man, sitting on chair is me only", I said. "What? You have long hair and you are very fat too", she exclaimed. "Yeah, I am", I replied. She angrily put the call off. I was mute for sometime on hearing that. My heart beat increased as I feared losing her. I called her in afternoon. She said, "I don"t want to talk to you, you are a liar". Those words brought tears in my eyes. I made a plan. She gave a miss call in the evening but I didn"t respond. Next day I messaged her that I got ill in the evening and was in hospital for the whole night. I called her many times but she didn"t respond. Finally, she responded and asked me to call after 10 at night. I was very anxious. It was a cold winter night and I was on my roof top at 10 in night. I called her and her first reaction was very disturbing for me. I was shocked. 42 "You liar………..think what you have done, broken my trust, I have decided not to continue any type of relation with you, I trusted you and you have done this to me" then she started weeping. I was feeling guilty and said, "Dear I did not intend to hurt you but feared losing you. I was also aware of your disliking for fatty people that"s why I did not tell you the truth. You don"t know how much I love you. I will die without you". She replied in anger, "Ok, fine. I agree that you do not want to lose me as you are fat, but you lied to me that you were in the hospital that day but me, Shivali and her fiancé saw you at your brother"s office that evening. Don"t you think of me and my love for you while lying about these things to me" and started weeping again. "No dear, I was feeling very insecure after you saw me as I judged on talking to you that you didn"t like me" I replied with tears. "I don"t want to talk to you any more, this is my last call to you", she said angrily. I begged her, "Don"t do this to me dear, I will certainly die without your love. I will do whatever you want. I will lose my weight at any cost, please be with me, I beg of you". "I am not so generous. Firstly I agreed to compromise on your problem and now this. I lost my father few years back; I want someone who can support me. This situation is so painful for me that the person whom I loved and trusted has broken it. I want to die, I want to die", she cried in tears. "I beg of you dear, don"t do that I will also die without you. I will do whatever you want. Please forgive me", I replied. We both were in tears, after some time she said, "I need time to take decision and I will tell you tomorrow that what is to be done about our relation and so called love", and then she cut the call. It was a matter of life and death for me. My tears were unstoppable as I did not know the destiny of my love. Whole night I was thinking of ending my life if I had to be without my love. I was cursing God for everything. 43 Next day I called her, "Hi dear, how are you?" in a very emotional voice. She replied, "I don"t want to talk to you, you played with my feelings, what I can do now, I want to die," "No dear, I will die without you but please give me one more chance, I will reduce my weight in 3 months, I promise." After lot of arguments she agreed but on a condition that I send my recent photographs to her. I saw a ray of hope. I was out looking for a photographer and within one hour I did send her the photographs. Then I called her, "Hi dear, did you see the photographs?" She started weeping loudly and asked, "Why have you done this to me, I don"t see any happiness in my life, I lost my father, I trusted you after him and you betrayed me. I will not bear this thing, I will certainly die". I was also in tears and asked her, "Please tell me what has happened, I have sent the photographs to you, have you seen them? She replied, "It seems that this is the photograph of any Dracula with long hairs". I pleaded, "Dear, I will get them cut for you and send you the photographs.

Though I am fat yet I am smart". "Smart!!! hmmm, good joke" she replied sarcastically. "Ok I will send you the photograph tomorrow" I said. I never wanted to cut the hair I had grown over the last six months. My mother asked me many times to get them cut but I didn"t listen to her and did not want anyone to interfere in that as long hairs were my passion. But now my love was at stake so I decided to sacrifice my long grown hairs. I was very much sad on seeing them cut and falling on floor. I did send my photograph to her. She got relaxed on seeing that and commented, "You are looking like a human now but yesterday you looked like an animal". I got angry on hearing that but didn"t react. I thought that if it is only the physical appearance which matters to her and not my feeling then my endless love may have no value for her. But I was addicted to her love, her talks and it was very hard for me to give up that addiction. But I got relaxed that she would be with me after the sacrifices which I was doing for her. She elucidated it one by one. 44 "You should keep short hair". "You should do exercise and yoga everyday". "You have to control your diet, no high calorie food, no breakfast only salad, in lunch only two chapattis with curd, in dinner only two chapattis with boiled dal". The biggest sacrifice which I made was of tea, as I was addicted to taking nearly 10 cups of tea a day but as per strict book of rules framed by my beloved I was supposed to take two cups of tea a day and that too without sugar. For one addiction (her love) I had to give up other ones. The most important of the rules was to send my photographs to her every fortnight for the evaluation of my performance and then I had to bear the result in the form of her happiness or annoyance which depended on my performance. I decided to obey the regulations rigorously. When I was about to leave Jammu in a day or so, she called me and said, "Show me the result in two three months otherwise I would be out of your life, and then don"t try to make me emotional. You will have to change your physique. I see many people on airport but no one looks like you. I want you to be of such a physique that everyone gets impressed on seeing. What about your treatment, are you going to Amritsar tomorrow for the check up?" I was little disturbed, as I had lied to her that I was following the advice taken Amritsar for my treatment as I left following the same 5 years ago. I lied again, "Yes dear, off course, I am going tomorrow for treatment". I was little disturbed with her behavior but thought that every girl has the right to choose the best for her as her partner; she was trying to do that only. I was also excited that she was taking full interest in me. One day before I had to leave Jammu, my younger brother read messages sent by her and now my family came to know about her. They tried to ask many questions but I did not them anything. Next day, I left Jammu at 5 AM she called me at 6 and said, "Take care of yourself and follow the diet as I have told you. Also make sure to follow the doctor in Amritsar, bye". I didn"t know what to say as one problem or the other was there which I had to solve. But I left everything on destiny. She called me and asked, "Where are you dear?" 45 "I have reached Amritsar dear and taking medicine". I lied to her. She got suspicious and asked, "Tell me the distance which you have travelled and how could you reach there so soon". I got angry and said, "Why don"t you trust me at all. I am doing all this for your sake and still you doubt me." Then she asked in an emotional tone, "I know you are there for me dear, you talk to the doctor and then take food. I will talk to you in evening". I was feeling culpable as I had lied to her again but it was better to lie than to be in pain. I was looking bit slim and everyone in my hostel was amazed on seeing that. I got up early in the morning with great excitement and even sometimes my beloved used to call me to wake me up. Sometimes my friends forced me to take butter or high calories food, but I never took as I was fully in her love and left all those things for her. Her love was more important for me than other pleasures of life. I was feeling great exhilaration in my life. I was filled with great vitality and enthusiasm. I took care of my health well not for me but for my beloved. I was feeling as if some mystical vigor would do all things and I was filled with great energy. She instructed me what to eat and what not to and I followed those instructions with great zeal. She acted as a perfect guide. I used to send her the photographs every 15 days as directed by her so that she can make out how much weight I had lost. But sometimes I asked myself that is it true love but then convinced myself that she cared for me. I had a great trust in her, even more than myself. This continued for weeks and I was looking slim and handsome   now.

****

CHAPTER EIGHT

MY OBSESSION GREW WEAKER

I not only loved her but was greatly obsessed with her love. Whenever she talked about her marriage I got highly disturbed as even the thought of that shivered me. She often insisted me to do something about my health as otherwise she would get married somewhere else. But I only gave her assurance. Sometimes I wondered whether she really loved me or not? In hostel we used to enjoy a lot and even my love story was known to everyone as I was always occupied with her calls and thoughts. My friend, Anil whose sister was Sonia"s colleague often insisted me to leave her as she didn"t love me. One day Sonia"s colleague Sujata who happened to be Anil"s friend talked to Anil at night. A cunning idea came into my mind as in hostel boys often used to make fun with each other. After Anil and Sujata finished their chat I messaged Sujata from his mobile, "I love you dear, I love you more than anything else, I can"t live without you". Then I deleted the message from the list of sent items. After sometime Anil asked me about that but I out rightly denied that I had sent any message. He asked me many times as he doubted that I might have sent some vulgar message to her. On being asked repeatedly I told him about the message I had sent. But he didn"t agree to that. He still doubted and warned me of the dire consequences in anger. Next day I got a call from Sonia, "I don"t want to continue my relation with you anymore". I asked in distress, "What happened dear?" "I wanted you to meet everyone in my office as my future husband, but now you have downgraded your reputation as Anil"s sister has told me many things about you which are very disgusting and I don"t like such a person to be my husband". I was very much worried as I had never done such a thing. I enquired about that. Finally she told me, "Anil"s sister has told everyone in my office about you and about your health also. Everyone asks me about you. She has also told that we meet frequently and that you have sent some vulgar message to Sujata. Everyone is asking me about all this. You lied to Anil about our relation. Tell me where we met. I don"t want to continue my relation with a liar". 47 "Dear, I never said this to Anil. He does not get well along with me and it a lie made by Anil, please try to understand me". "No, I don"t want any relation with you" she said angrily and put the call off. I was in tears as didn"t know how to convince her and I feared losing her. I could not sleep that night and next day tried to contact her but she didn"t take my calls. I was in distress for next three days. It was affecting my studies but at that time the most important matter for me was my love and not my studies. I was not able to perform my routine work even. I begged of her many times. Finally she put one condition that I should call her when I would be alright and not before that. It was very hard for me. I begged of her then at last she agreed on the condition that Sujata and Anil"s sister should apologize in front of everyone and confess that whatever they said was a lie. It was hard for me but somehow I convinced Anil to make Sujata to do that. But now I was fed up with all those things. I had to give explanation for everything. What was my fault that I had a physical problem? Didn"t I have the right to be loved? Sometimes I felt that she talked to me just out of pity for me. I was feeling as if I was living on her mercy. I came to know through Anil that Sonia told Sujata that she didn"t love me. She talked to me simply because she pitied me and feared that I would do something unusual if she stopped talking to me. I was really fed up. I discussed with my friends Satnam and Praveen about that. They suggested me to give her up as I was playing with my future for the sake of a girl who never loved me but was just passing her time. So I decided that I would try to make a distance from her and rather try to divert my mind towards my studies. So, I reduced the frequency of talking to her. I wanted to get rid of the addiction of talking to her. It was very difficult for me but somehow I was successful in that as I was aware of the fact that one day or other she would be out of my life.

****

****

CHAPTER NINE

FIRST DATE WITH MY EXTRA LOVE AFFAIR

"True love never dies, even if you have found a new love, the sweet memory of the past will continue to hunt you for the rest of your life". It is a well-known theory of flirt people that if you love two persons at a time and one leaves you then you have other to soothe you. Going by the same, one of my friends offered his estranged girlfriend, Deepika to me. I was hesitant at first but then I started talking to her. But whenever I talked to her I felt guilty for Sonia that I was playing with her feelings. But affair with Deepika was without any emotions on my part. It was the summer break in the month of June. I decided to spend it with my family at home. I had made plans for meeting Deepika. So, when I reached home I called her and expressed my desire to meet her. At first, she declined but after my insistence she agreed to meet me but decided that we would not talk to each other, only see each other. We decided the place to meet. I reached there fifteen minutes before the decided time. She went to a shop and asked for something, then came back. For whole of the time, she continuously stared at at me and my eyes were also on her. Then after coming out of the shop, she asked, "Are you Sameer?". " I said, "Yeah, I am and you Deepika?". She gave a smile and started moving. "When will you come to meet me". I asked her. "May be tomorrow" she replied and then she went away. She was a beautiful lady with long hair and I liked her simplicity though she was elder to me which was obvious on by her looks. That night we had a conversation on phone. She really liked me and asked about the type of dress I liked. I told her about my likings dislIking"s. We decided to meet next day in a restaurant near my house. I was feeling excited but at the same time there was guilt in a corner of my heart for Sonia whom I loved the most. The guilt was that I was cheating Sonia. But then I thought I was not at all emotionally attached to her. At 2 in the afternoon I got ready for my first date with my extra love affair. I was wearing my finest dress and perfume and left home at 2:30 PM for the date. After a wait 49 of 10 minutes, she was there. In those ten minutes I thought of the ways to convey my desire to her. She entered the restaurant. I offered her a seat beside me, "Hi Deepika, how are you?" She replied, "I am fine, what about you". She was in a white silky, sleeveless dress, with loose hairs and the makeup was used to hide her wrinkles, her face was oily. I was little disappointed on seeing her as I liked her simplicity the day before which was nowhere today. But she was a beautiful lady, a lady in early thirties. The waiter asked me about the order, "Hi Sir, what do you want to have?" I wanted to spend some time with her so I ordered sweet corn soup and a coffee as it would take

some time to prepare that. Then we had the normal conversation. Then I held her hand. She resisted. I again tried to hold but she again resisted with discontentment. Then without talking anything I had my soup and went away without uttering a word. She called me at night, "Hi Sameer, what happened to you today in restaurant?" "You know well", I replied with anger. "I got little angry and sorry for that but it was not right on your part to hold my hand on the first date". She said. "I know it was our first date but we are known to each other for the last 3 months. I was of the thought that we knew each well, don"t we?" I asked her furiously. "Yes but we had never ever met before, so how could a girl react on being touched by someone on first meeting. It was a natural reaction", she replied. "But I don"t like that; you don"t trust me". "Ok sorry for that, we will meet tomorrow, is that ok?", she said. "Ok", I replied. Next day we met at the same place and at same time. We had normal conversation and then I held her hand in the same way. She did not react. I kept holding her hand for two hours. I was feeling nothing as I was emotionally attached to Sonia. I really wanted to have an affair with her but after hearing her story I was moved and then decided not to play with her emotions. She was the youngest of the three sisters. Elder ones were married. She had to look after her old and ailing father. She worked to earn for 50 herself and her father and she wanted someone to marry her. After hearing that I didn"t have the courage to talk to her.
****
****

CHAPTER TEN

THE HEARTENING TALE OF CRUMBLE

"That which does not kill us will only make us stronger." - Friedrich Nietzsche Sonia started ignoring me, I didn"t know what the problem was and maybe she wanted to discontinue it. Sometimes she talked so strangely that it shivered me. May be she had an inkling that our relation would not last longer. May be she was being more realistic than me. It was the month of October 2007, the month of emotional ups and downs for me. The month when I lost someone very dear to me and gained something very important in life, the month when I got a new birth in life. I was very much desperate for her and frequently called her and she ignored me very much. I forced her to talk to her mother about our relation and we often quarreled upon that. I was of the view that family could never refuse if the person himself or herself is strong enough to convince them properly. But she said that she was scared of doing so and often asked me that do whatever I wanted to and she even threatened me that she would not recognize me if I sent a proposal at her place. This was very heartening for me as how could a person go ahead in relationship without any support from the other side. Our relation was struggling for survival now and I was collecting its ruins. She had to go to Delhi for training and she even didn"t tell me about that. I was quite depressed. She didn"t call me even while leaving for Delhi. I messaged her in anguish when she was about to leave, "Dear, I will die without you and that"s final and you will not see me anymore on being back to Jammu". In distress I called her friend Anu and told about the whole saga of my love to her. "Hi Anu, I am Sameer. Do you recognize me?" I asked her. "Yeah I know, you are Sonia"s friend, but why are you disturbing her again and again?" she replied furiously. "No dear, I love her very much and how could I disturb her?" I replied in a poignant tenor. "But she doesn"t love you, simply talking to someone is not love", she told me". I got furious over that, "How could you conclude that without knowing about our relation". 52 "Which relation????" she lamented angrily. "Ask your friend that what is going between us for the last one and half year" I asked her angrily. "She told me that both of you are just friends and there is nothing between the two of you", she said. I got furious over that and told her everything about our relation. She listened to that very patiently and was moved by our love. She said "If it is really like that then she is being very unfair to you and if she really loves you then she should stand by you in spite of your problem. I will talk to her, you need not worry". "I will definitely die without her. I only have a physical problem otherwise I am well educated and will definitely do well professionally" I told her with tears in eyes. "Don"t worry dear, I will talk to her and please think about your family and never ever think of ending your life. The thing for which you are crying now, Sonia cried for the same two years ago", she replied. I was astonished and asked, "What are you saying?" She replied, "Yes, she had a boyfriend two years ago and she cried like you as her boyfriend forced her for marriage and she responded the same as this time". I was furious and amazed upon that as she hid such a big thing from me and asked her, "Where the boy is working now?" "He is in Delhi now, engineer in a company. Caste was the issue at that time and she didn"t have the courage to talk to her family. I will definitely talk to her about you and if she really loves you then she should talk to her family. You don"t worry; think about your future and your family. I will talk to her, everything will be all right". She told me patiently. I got amazed over her hiding relation from me; I never ever expected this thing from her. The person who was there in my life for the last one and half year hid such a big thing from me. But after some time I soothed my mind that I would let her off for that. It was very heartening to know that your beloved had relations with somebody else which she did not disclose to you. But somehow I accepted that. 53 In distress I sent a mail to her friend, "Dear, please do something for our relation otherwise I will die". But unfortunately I was mistaken in writing the email id address and it went to the id of Anu"s colleague. They all made fun of that mail. She came back from Delhi after her training and her friend told her everything our conversation and about the mail also. Sonia gave a call to one of my relatives and told her that I was disturbing her by calling her. She also told that she was going to marry soon. My relative asked me about her. I got annoyed over that and called Sonia, "Hi Sonia, how are you? Your friend, Anu told me about your last affair but you didn"t tell me about that". She angrily said, "It is none of your business. I respected you but you have lost that respect now by telling these things to Anu and by sending mail. Everyone at Anu"s office is making fun of you. I don"t want to talk to a person like you anymore". I moaned in anguish, "Please don"t say these things to me. I was mistaken in writing the email id but whatever I said to Anu is true, you love me and I love you". "I don"t love you, who said that? I only talk to you simply because I feel pity for you and your health but now I don"t even have the mercy for a person like you. I don"t want to talk to you anymore. GET LOST and GO TO HELL." she said. A shower of tears started coming out of my eyes. I was feeling as if my world had ended. The dreams which I had seen with her seemed fake to me. I was feeling that she loved me for every good as well as bad thing in me but I did not know that this was her mercy for me. What about her love, care and promises made to me? That night was very stressful for me and I even thought of ending my life. For that purpose, I even got a knife from my friend"s room. That night I called her nearly for 1000 times on her phone and did not get even a second of sleep. Next day it was 15ᵗʰ October. I got up early and thanked God for everything that he had given me and also felt sorry to my family and friends. I decided of making it the last day of my life. I got the contact number of Sonia"s office and called her, "How are you?" 54 She started abusing me and said the things which I had never expected from her. Then she said something which was truly heartening for me. "I have a boyfriend and I don"t want you to be in darkness, we are going to be married in December" she said. "You are lying, I don"t believe that. You can"t do this to me. I am going to die, I will definitely die", I said with tears and pain. "Go to hell and do whatever you want to" she replied and cut the call. In anguish I brought knife near my wrist and was ready to die. In the meanwhile she called my brother and started complaining about me, "I am Sonia, I want to tell you something about your brother. He is calling me again and again even in my office. I don"t know him well and have never even seen him. He is forcing me to marry him; I am going to be married in December". My brother got angry over her behavior and said, "Now you are getting disturbed by his calls and what about the time when you used to call him for 20-30 times in a day. Didn"t you think even once that we might be getting disturbed by your calls? She got annoyed and said in anger, "You don"t know me. I will teach you a lesson". My brother replied rudely, "Ok, tell who you are". On hearing that she cut the call and called me angrily, "Hello, you don"t know me". I replied, "What has happened dear". "Your brother doesn"t know how to talk. I will break his bones" she said. With this sentence of her, whole of my love for her vanished. I could never bear the insult of my family at the hands of the person whom I knew for last few months only. "What are you saying? Mind your language", I asked while hurling the knife on the door angrily. She said in a taunting manner, "First learn how to walk then talk to me." I could not bear so harsh comments about my physical problem and said furiously, "What do you think of yourself? Are you very beautiful? Now hear the reality, when I saw you 55 for the first time, I could not sleep for nearly a week. You have a manly face and resemble a vampire." She got angry and said, "It was you who was mad for me. When I will get married, I will keep the persons like you to sweep the floor of my house" Then our arguments continued and I replied, "What do you think of yourself? Even my maid is more beautiful than you" On hearing that she put the call off and stopped taking my calls. After half an hour I called her from my friend"s mobile. She was in tears that time and I asked her not to show her crocodile tears to me. I wanted to make her realize what she had said. In the afternoon I again called her from a PCO booth and heated arguments continued. Then finally she showed her behavior once again and started commenting on my family. Lastly I said, "Look, I doesn"t know your family well and also my family values doesn"t allow me to utter such words for anyone. But finally I know the reality of your thinking and attitude. It"s my last call to you and I thank God that he saved me from being ruined by marrying a person like you otherwise my life would have become a hell." With this last stroke on her behavior I put off the call. That was finally my breakup day. I wanted to celebrate my breakup day with my friends. We celebrated it with two bottles of Antiquity (whiskey), some bottles of beer, chicken and we danced all night. It was really the Independence Day for me. Though we had a party but there was a pain in my heart   because   of   break   up   with   her.

****
****

CHAPTER ELEVEN

The rise of devil in me and my hypothetical beloved

"Love is as much of an object as an obsession, everybody wants it, everybody seeks it, but few ever achieve it, those who do will cherish it, be lost in it, and among all, never... never forget it". Curtis Judalet The next day was so devastating for me that it would be impossible to describe that. I got up early in the morning at 5:00 AM which was unusual for me. I took bath and heard the shlokas of Gita to soothe my mind. I felt a little bit relaxed. I got ready for the college, didn"t want to eat anything. I felt like crying but somehow managed to stop the tears from coming out in front of my friends and pretended to smile. But I cried whenever I was alone because I was feeling as if someone had taken away a part of my body. The pain of solitude was very devastating, even more than the death of a loved one as one does not see the dead person again but in my case the person whom I loved more than anything else left me and I could see the person but with somebody else. Seeing the person you love with another is very painful. I thought of her only and her so called boyfriend about whom she had told me on my breakup day. I didn"t know if it was a reality or fake. I was thinking that how a person who loved me so much could do such thing to me. I tried to soothe my mind by convincing myself that she had no boyfriend. 16th October was an unusual day for me. I did not expect her calls now and I was also not going to call her. That day I wore finest of my clothes. Everyone of my class knew about the party last night. It was a break up party, very unusual for anyone. Everyone including the girls was very polite to me. One of my friends passed a comment about my dress, "Sameer, What is the reason of wearing this fine dress? Last day was your break up day and today this dress!!!" "Now I am in search of a new girlfriend", I uttered these words with a fake smile and frown heart. In the evening I was back in my hostel and cried in darkness for about half an hour. After that I was in my bed without any food and water, had a small sleep. When I opened my eyes, there were again tears and then I slept again. That went on for two three days. 57 My friends Satnam and Praveen knew about my situation well. They tried to soothe my mind. They tried hard to make me happy and were always with me in college as well as hostel. They feared that I might harm myself in the state of depression. But strangely my concentration in studies improved as I wanted to prove to her that I was not a worthless chap which she had tried to made me feel on my breakup day. But every day I missed her and cried for her. The pain of loneliness was consuming me day by day but somehow I tried to appease my mind. I lost everything in life. I left following all my treatments, yoga and everything which I had done for her love. I was feeling weakness and my condition worsened day by day as I was having sleepless nights without any food and water. I thought about her only, the time spent with her, the promises made by her, her smile, her possessive for me, her love for me, and her care for me. Loneliness and rejection hurts a person very much. My life was totally devastated; my condition worsened day by day. I gave up all the medicines and treatment which I had been taking because of her love and started drinking frequently to soothe my mind After 6 days I got a call, "Hi Sameer, how are you?" "May I know who you are?" I asked. "Make a guess", she said. "Your voice is not familiar to me. Please tell me", I replied with a frown. "Keep guessing, keep guessing, I will not tell you about that", she replied with a giggle. "I am already in distressing stage, please tell me who you are" I asked her furiously. "Ok, I give you a clue, we were very close friends in school days" she told. "I still don"t remember you, my memory is short lived" I replied. "Ok, I give you another clue. I proposed you two years ago and you said that you are a one woman man and that woman you have alreadyd found" she said. "Oh, I remember now, it"s Mitali. Where were you? I did not expect a call from you." I exclaimed. "You forgot your dear friend; I have not expected this thing at least from you. I know you have your love with you but good friends are always an asset. Please 58 spare some love for your friends also. It"s good that you love your girlfriend but don"t be so much occupied in her love only", she said. I started crying loudly on hearing that. She asked me, "What has happened dear? Why are you crying so much?" "How can I tell you dear that I lost everything in my life? I lost my love and I will certainly die without her" "No dear, you are a very brave man, tell me what happened" she asked. I told her the whole story and she listened to it very patiently. She was moved by my tale of love. At the end she told me, "Sameer, in life there comes certain situations when a person feels like giving up but those are coward ones. You are a very brave boy and I think you can overcome this pain. Think about future". Mitali was my school time friend and more than a friend for me. She was from Shimla. Her father was a civil servant. After her school, her family had shifted to Delhi. After completing her studies she got a job with a software company in Bangalore. Since our school days she had special feelings for me. She was even aware about my health condition. In November 2006 she even proposed me and I told her that I was a one woman man and I had found that woman in my life. But Mitali still loved me. She started making frequent calls to me so as to make me feel happy and relaxed but I used to be drunk daily which hurt her very much as she cared for me. I always talked about Sonia, her care and her love. Though I hated Sonia due to her behavior on the last day of our relationship yet I loved her as I was unable to forget the love and care which I got from her. I also thought sometimes that Sonia might have done all that to me because her family was conservative and they might not have agreed for our relation. On other moment I wondered that why she didn"t take any initiative to talk to her family and on the last day she went to the extent of saying that she felt pity on me. On one evening I got a call from Mitali, "Hi Sameer, how are you?" I was in

drunken stage and started crying. Mitali said, "
Sameer, I don"t want to see you like this. I have
decided something and I want to convey it to you
whether you like it or not but I have to". "What dear?"
I asked. 59 "Though you may think that I am
opportunist but I want to hold your hand and walk
with you, for the rest of my life dear. I want to marry
you" she said in an emotional tone. "Dear you know
about my condition and my health problem is more
severe than what it was in our school days" I replied.
"I don"t know anything. I only know that I love you
and love is not about physical appearance or anything
like that, it"s a bond of two souls and I don"t want my
love to vanish in distress. I will talk to my father and
they know your family well so there is no problem in
that." she said. That day I realized that Mitali loved
me a lot which I had never ever expected. On one
side, it was Mitali who knew everything about me and
was ready to accept me with all that and on other
side, it was Sonia who tried to make me feel that she
would be ashamed of me as her boyfriend. What sort
of love was that????????????????? But it also
showed that she cared for me and that is why kept on
pressing me for my treatment. All these thoughts
brought tears in my eyes. But at the same time I hated
her for talking badly about my family and hiding about
her previous relation from me. "Take the revenge
from her as she played with your feelings. She has
provoked you so much that you have almost taken
your life. Give her a lesson so that never ever a person
ditches anyone in love, never disregard anyone"s
family and never make false promises. Make her
realize that what she has lost in life, tell her about

Mitali, marry Mitali and make her jealous of that as it is the most depressing to see a person whom you love with someone else. " devil in me said to me and I decided to tie the knot with Mitali even though I didn"t love her but I decided to use her love to make Sonia realize what she had lost. Mitali was like my imaginary beloved. Though she loved me but for me she was a good friend not more than that. She called me every day and sometimes I compared her to Sonia and then used to be in tears as for me Sonia was the most lovable person and no one else could be in her place. When you give that special place in your heart to anyone else, you always miss her, her love and her talks. This void in life cannot be filled by anyone and it remains as such for the whole life. My personality was split at that particular moment. 60 "I love you so much and I want you back in my life at any cost. I want to fulfill the promises made by me. I want to live my life with you. I will work hard to fulfill your expectations. I want you back." eudemon in me suggest me to do that. "You have to take revenge of your sufferings and what she has done to you. You have to make her realize what she has lost. Get married to Mitali and invite her to your marriage which will be most distressing for her. Come on, you have to do that", devil in me compelled met. But demon overpowered eudemon and I decided to go on the way the demon took me to. I got a recent photograph of Mitali and mailed it to Sonia with a small wording. "Hi, this is my girlfriend Mitali. She was my school time friend and now we have decided to tie the knot" I wanted to tell her friend the reason of our breakup and how she disregarded my family. So I sent a mail to her friend Anu telling her the reason of our breakup. Dear Anu, I don"t know what Sonia has told you about me but we love each other very much. I have done everything for her as she felt that I should get myself treated for my health problem otherwise it would not be good for both of us. She even cried sometimes and I have done everything for her. I got Rs.5000 as scholarship, out of which I spent nearly Rs.4000 for my treatment; I even took steroids to improve my condition. But I think everything is in vain. I was crazy about the person who has no respect for me family. Thank God I have come to know about her before our marriage otherwise me and my family would have been in trouble. I want to tell her the truth related to our relation and her true nature. God has taken me out of her clutches. Thank God and also tell her I have found the right person in my life. May good sense prevail in her. With Regards, Sameer. 61 Anu was her good friend and even the misunderstanding between us started when I told her about our relation, and she was of the view that if she really loved me then she would stand by me in all the circumstances. I wanted to tell her about the misbehavior of her friend. After two days of sending the mail, I got a call, "Hi, I want to talk to you". "I don"t recognize you, can you please tell me who are you?" I asked. "I am Sonia and want to ask you that why did you send mail to Anu? Don"t send any mail to her in future." she said and the put the call off. I was busy at that moment so didn"t talk much to her. After half an hour I called her. "Hi, I did send mail to Anu to tell her that what her friend have done with me and the way she disregarded my family", I said furiously. She got angry over that and said, "But why don"t you understand that he also talked badly to me". "But no one has any right to disregard my family and now I have a girlfriend. My school time friend proposed me and I accepted it. She loves me very much". I replied. She was almost in tears, "She would not stay for more than six months with you. God is seeing everything and will teach you a lesson for what all you did to me". "God has seen everything that who has played with whose feelings. You pretended to love me but in front of everyone said that you talked to me because of mercy for me", I asked her wrathfully. "Who are you? Who loves you? You are nobody in my life", she said these words angrily and put off the call. I was annoyed but also started crying as I loved her more than anything else but at the same time didn"t want anyone to disregard my family also. After talking to her, I felt that she wanted to reconcile and wanted to make up our estranged relation but I missed that opportunity because of clash of our egos. I lost the first opportunity of making with her and relation between us was even bitterer. That night I was in quite distressing stage, I told Mitali about everything and she tried to soothe my mind. She decided to talk to her father as early as possible as I was in abysmal pain of rejection. Next day she talked to her father and decided to get engaged in 62 December after my brother"s marriage. But as Sonia"s love was still fresh in my mind, I decided not to marry for two more years in disguise of preparation of civil services. In distress eudemon in me forced me to send message to Sonia, "I and Mitali have decided to get engaged in December" After some days Mitali called me and said, "Dear, today is karwachauth and I decided to keep fast for you today". "Dear, please don"t fast this time as it"s very heartening to give Sonia"s place to anyone else". I started crying and remembered the last year"s Karvachauth with her. On karvachauth, women keep a fast wishing long life of their husbands. Though we had broken up but I could still feel the warmth of the last year"s Karvachauth. She had called me at 4 in the morning; in fact it was to let me know that she was awake. I asked, "Dear, you have call me so early in the morning, is anything urgent?" She replied, "No but I was awake at 4 as today is karvachauth. All women are awake to take meal; next year I will celebrate this at your home". I replied in a poignant mood, "Are you fasting today for me". She replied, "I wanted to keep fast for you dear but what will I tell my family members that for whom I am fasting and they may get suspicious about me but when we will be together I will wake up and keep fast for you". "Ok dear, I will also not eat and drink anything and take the meals with you only at night". I replied. She giggled and said, "Let"s see dear". Though we were apart but emotionally we had tied the knot. The warmth of her words was still fresh in my mind and I was in tears seeing any girl celebrating karvachauth. This is the occasion which depicts a wife"s devotion for her husband when she fasts wishing for her husband"s long life and takes food only at night after seeing her husband. It reminded me of her endless love for me who was ready to perform all the rituals which a wife would perform for her husband in an Indian culture. 63 On the occasion of Diwali, I had a strong desire to talk to her but did not know what to talk. My brother"s marriage was due soon so I decided to talk to her in disguise of asking about air fares for going to Bangalore. I called her, "Hi, how are you?" She recognized me immediately and said, "I am fine. How are you?" "Just alive. I want to ask you the fares for Bangalore as I have to send invitation of my brother"s marriage to my friend", I said. "There is no direct flight to Bangalore. I suggest you not to send it by air". She replied. "You also have to come to my brother"s marriage along with your mother" I invited her. "Ok, I will try to come, mail me the invitation card. When is your engagement?" she asked. "May be in December but not sure, may be after two years as I have to prepare for civil services", I replied. "Will she wait for you?" she asked with tears. "She proposed me, not I. She loves me. So if she wants to marry to me, she will have to wait" I replied. "You tell when are you going to marry and how is your boyfriend? What he does?" I asked her sarcastically. She replied, "He is fine". "What he does?" I again asked her. She was almost in tears while replying, "He works somewhere" and then she put the call off. She was hiding her pain from me but how could I be unaware of that as I loved her and could feel her pain. That day I judged that she had no boyfriend and was experiencing the same pain that I experienced on breakup day. It"s very painful when you know that a person you love meant for you is going to be in someone else life. We both loved each other but no one was going to take the initiative of reconciliation and this was the second chance to reconcile and makeup our estranged relation and we lost it. 64 After some days Mitali was out to Singapore with her father. I wanted to present a gift to my brother on his marriage. I called Sonia to take suggestion from her regarding the gift but the actual reason was that I wanted to talk to her. "Hi, how are you dear?" I asked her. "Fine but why have you called me?" she asked me. "I want to give a present to my brother on his marriage and I want you to give some suggestion." I said. "Ask your girlfriend, Mitali", she said furiously. "She has gone to Singapore with her father so I thought of taking suggestion form you, being a good friend." I replied. "I don"t know where she has gone but ask her and not me. I am not your girlfriend", she said in a low tone and put the call off. The demon in me was contented as he judged that she was really envious of Mitali which was quite obvious from her words. That night I kept on thinking about her and all the moments spent with her and was in tears. Though I had Mitali with me but whenever I talked to her, the memories of Sonia haunted me. I was feeling a void in my life. Things went on like that. Now it was the marriage season and my brother was also going to be married and I wanted to invite Sonia also. I called her, "Hi Sonia, how are you?" "Why have you called me?" she replied furiously. "I want to invite you for my brother"s marriage, my friend will give you the invitation card" I told her. "My boyfriend does not want me to continue any type of relation with you and don"t ever call me as usually I go out with him after office timings" She told me. I got little disturbed but decided to let her go and do whatever she wanted to. Though I was missing her on my brother"s marriage but I had reconciled believing it to be my destiny. After my brother"s marriage I was really stressed out. I was missing her so called her but her mobile phone was busy. Many thoughts came to my mind that she might be talking to 65 her boyfriend. It made me jealous. In a rage I messaged her to threaten her that I would end my life if she didn"t keep relation with me. It was the end of December. At around 12 in night I messaged her and I really did that. It was the foolishness on part of any lover but I really did that. My friends knocked the door in the morning and when I didn"t respond, they broke it down and were shocked to see blood all over in the room as I had cut my wrists. Next week was crucial for my life as I was in coma. When I regained consciousness every one of my family was in front of me and I was feeling sorry for them and also a rage for Sonia. It took me nearly a month to recover from it. I was a changed man after that with no love for anyone as the grave realities of human beings were known to me. But whenever I was drunk I called on Sonia"s number. Things kept on moving like that and months passed. In the mid of April, I got a call from a person who called himself to be Sonia"s fiancé and asked me about our relation? He also said that if I loved her then he would give up the idea of marrying her. In rage I told her the whole story and asked him to marry her as I didn"t have any love left for her. Next day I called Sonia and told her that I didn"t want to interfere in her matters, she could do whatever she wanted to do and could marry anyone she wanted to. I also told her not to call me ever again. Then she started abusing me and asked, "If I look like a vampire then what you look like?" I gave a laugh and told her, "I don"t have so much energy left to talk to you and please leave me as you don"t deserve me" She got furious over that and said, "What you think you are?" "I am the most stupid boy who was in love with a girl having ruthless attitude, narrow mind and many more things which I don"t want to say and also don"t ask your fiancé to call me again. I am totally fed up with you and your bloody emotional blackmailing and dramas and finally GET LOST AND OUT OF MY LIFE" I told her and finally decided not to talk to her again. It is a general perception of the lovers that if relation is to be broken the person who says these words (as said by me) is the winner and as I did that, I was feeling like a winner. Later on I came to know that it was a call from her colleague and it seemed that she 66 wanted to mend the relation with me but I had gone far away from her and decided not to be again in such a hell. "The hottest love has the coldest end" Socrates

The Step Of A True Angel In My Life

Sonia is married to her colleague and is working in Delhi. Mitali is a software engineer, working in Bangalore, is married and has a son also. I and Mitali talk to each other and are still good friends. After completing my studies, I worked in India"s reputed university as a lecturer for around a year. In this period of one year I found myself. After teaching for one year, I got selected in India"s premier institute, IIT (Indian institute of technology) for research. In my first week there, I met a girl on a matrimonial site. She was beautiful, intelligent and well qualified. She was working as a banker. I contacted her so as to proceed further for marriage and we started talking to each other. She was a beautiful human being and we developed liking and love for each other. I told her about all my previous stories and affairs. She accepted me with all those things and promised to give me so much love that I would forget all the sorrows of my life. Though I initially lied to her about my drinking and eating habits but later told her the truth. She accepted everything without any hesitation and finally we decided to get married. We got married in mid of the year 2011. Now we are a happy family, where love is all around and with her love I forgot all the old tragedies of my life. As said in bible "Love is patient, love is kind. It does not envy, it does not boast, it is not proud. It is not rude, it is not self-seeking, it is not easily angered, it keeps no record of wrongs. Love does not delight in evil, but rejoices with the truth. It always protects, always trusts, always hopes, always perseveres. Love never fails." Loneliness hurts. Rejection hurts. Losing someone hurts. Envy hurts. Everyone gets these things confused with love, but in reality love is the only thing in this world that covers up all pain and makes someone feel wonderful again. Love is the only thing in this world that does not hurt. *****************END******************